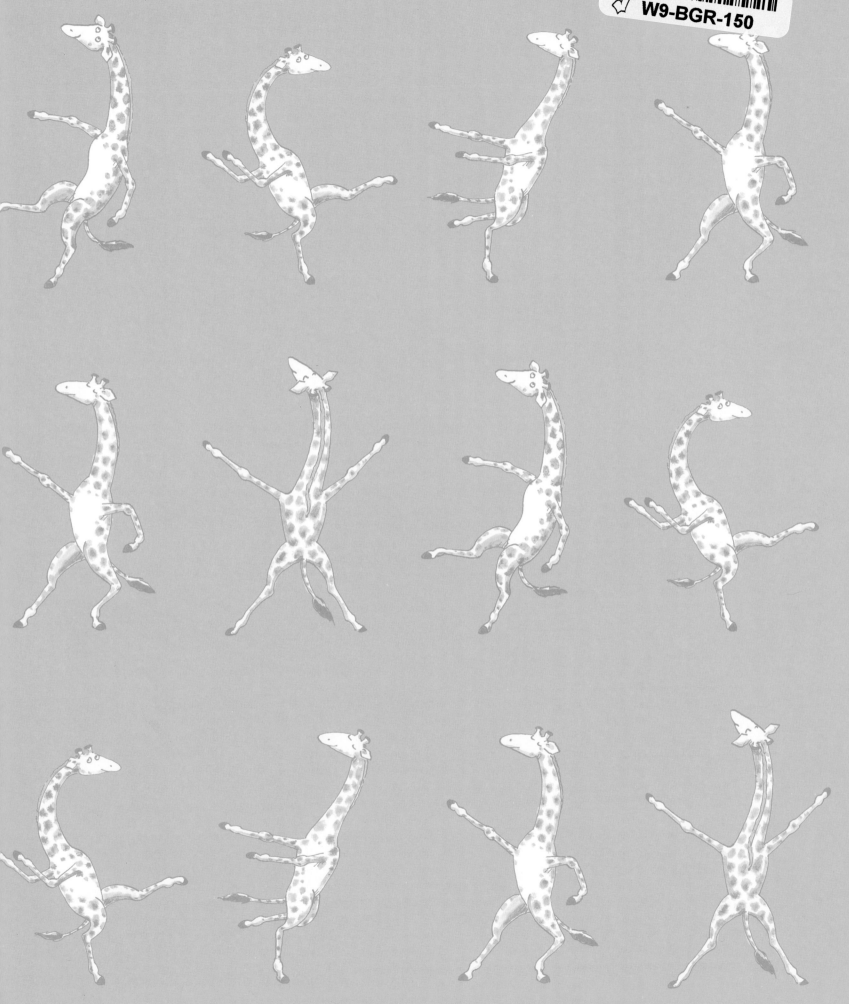

GIRAFFES CAN'T DANCE

To my cousins at Sandbanks – Giles
For Fi, John, Rod, and Andy – Guy

Text copyright © 1999 by Purple Enterprises Ltd
Illustrations copyright © 1999 by Guy Parker-Rees
First American edition 2001 published by Orchard Books
First published in Great Britain in 1999 by Orchard Books London

Giles Andreae and Guy Parker-Rees reserve the right to be identified as the author and the illustrator of this work.

Library of Congress Cataloging-in-Publication Data Available

The text of this book is set in Minion Condensed. The illustrations are watercolor and pen and ink.

This special edition was printed for Kohl's Department Stores, Inc. (for distribution on behalf of Kohl's Cares, LLC, its wholly owned subsidiary) by Scholastic Inc.

Kohl's
0-545-45840-4
123386
03/12

ISBN 978-0-545-45840-5

10 9 8 7 6 5 4 3 2 1   11 12 13 14 15 16/0

Printed in China   127
This edition first printing, March 2012

GIRAFFES CAN'T DANCE

by Giles Andreae
illustrated by Guy Parker-Rees

Orchard Books • New York
An Imprint of Scholastic Inc.

Gerald was a tall giraffe
whose neck was long and slim.
But his knees were awfully crooked
and his legs were rather thin.

He was very good at standing still
and munching shoots off trees.

But when he tried to run around,

he buckled at the knees.

Now every year in Africa
they hold the Jungle Dance,
where every single animal
turns up to skip and prance.

JUNGLE DANCE

And this year when the day arrived
poor Gerald felt so sad,
because when it came to dancing
he was really very bad.

The warthogs started waltzing

and the rhinos rock 'n' rolled.

The lions danced a tango
that was elegant and bold.

The chimps all did a cha-cha
with a very Latin feel,

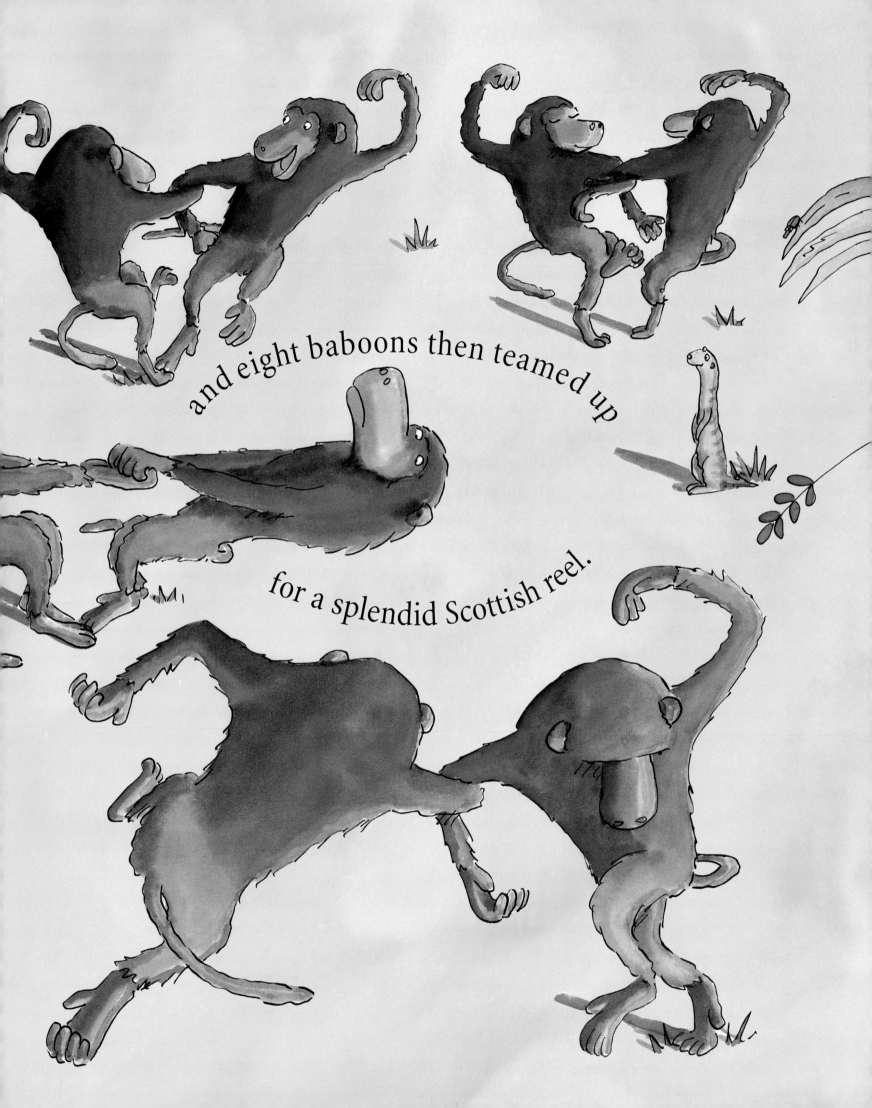

and eight baboons then teamed up for a splendid Scottish reel.

Gerald swallowed bravely
as he walked toward the floor.
But the lions saw him coming,
and they soon began to roar.

"Hey, look at clumsy Gerald,"
the animals all sneered.
"Giraffes can't dance, you silly fool!
Oh, Gerald, you're so weird."

Gerald simply froze up.

He was rooted to the spot.

They're right, he thought. *I'm useless.*

Oh, I feel like such a clot.

So he crept off from the dance floor,
and he started walking home.
He'd never felt so sad before—
so sad and so alone.

Then he found a little clearing,
and he looked up at the sky.
"The moon can be so beautiful,"
he whispered with a sigh.

"Excuse me!" coughed a cricket
who'd seen Gerald earlier on.
"But sometimes when you're different
you just need a different song."

"Listen to the swaying grass
and listen to the trees.
To me the sweetest music
is those branches in the breeze.

So imagine that the lovely moon
is playing just for you—
everything makes music
if you really want it to."

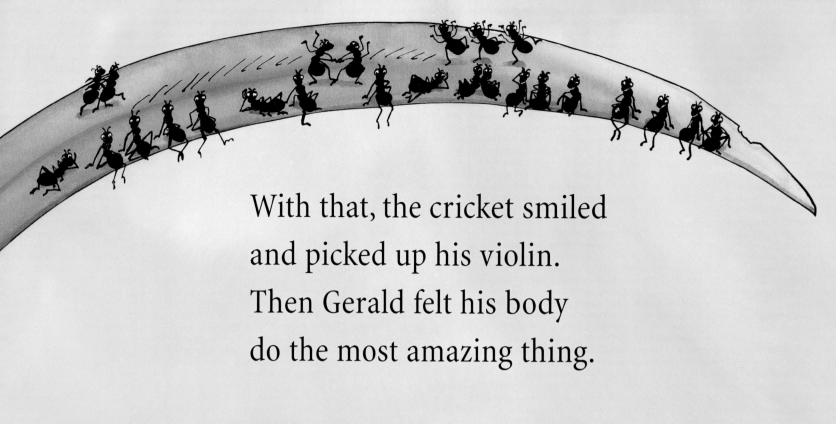

With that, the cricket smiled
and picked up his violin.
Then Gerald felt his body
do the most amazing thing.

His hooves had started shuffling,
making circles on the ground.
His neck was gently swaying,
and his tail was swishing round.

He threw his legs out sideways,
and he swung them everywhere.
Then he did a backward somersault
and leapt up in the air.

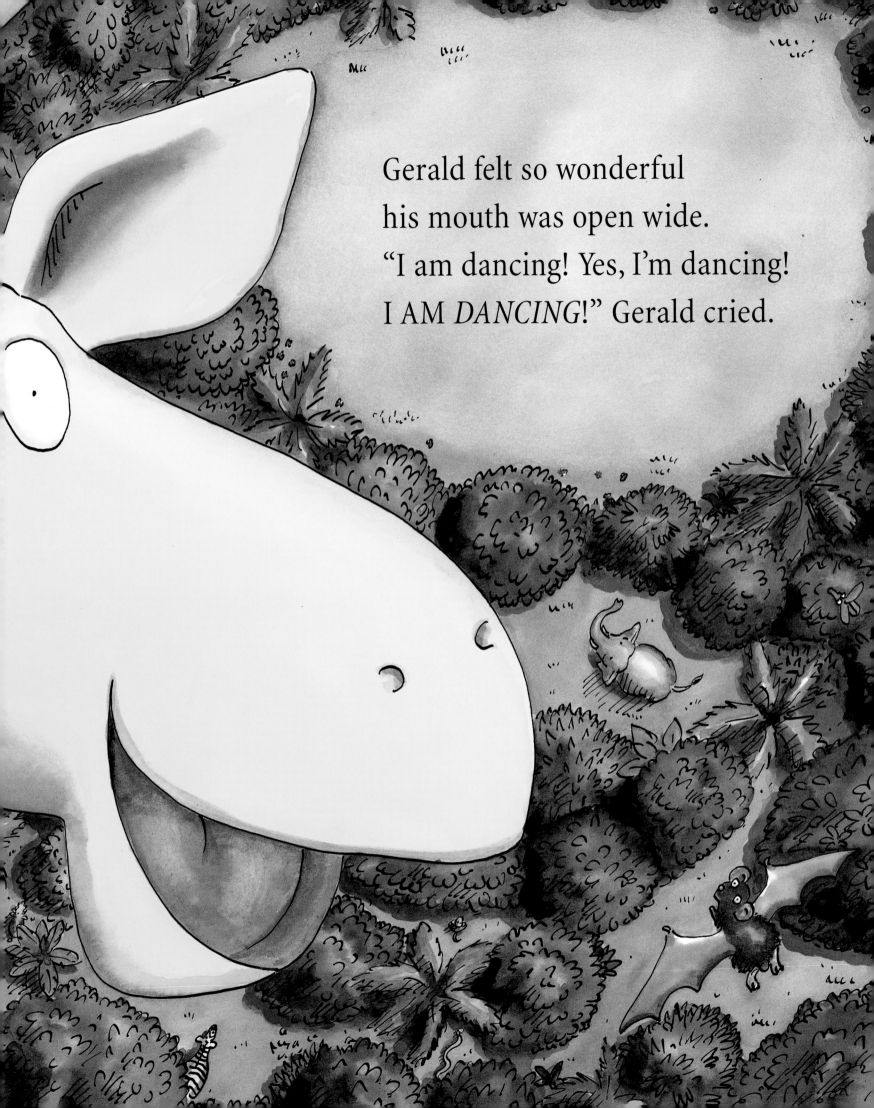

Gerald felt so wonderful
his mouth was open wide.
"I am dancing! Yes, I'm dancing!
I AM *DANCING*!" Gerald cried.

Then, one by one, each animal
who'd been there at the dance
arrived while Gerald boogied on
and watched him, quite entranced.

They shouted, "It's a miracle!
We must be in a dream.
Gerald's the best dancer
that we've ever, ever seen!"

"How did you learn to dance like that?
Please, Gerald, tell us how."
But Gerald simply twirled around
and finished with a bow.

Then he raised his head and looked up
at the moon and stars above.
"We all can dance," he said,
"when we find music that we love."

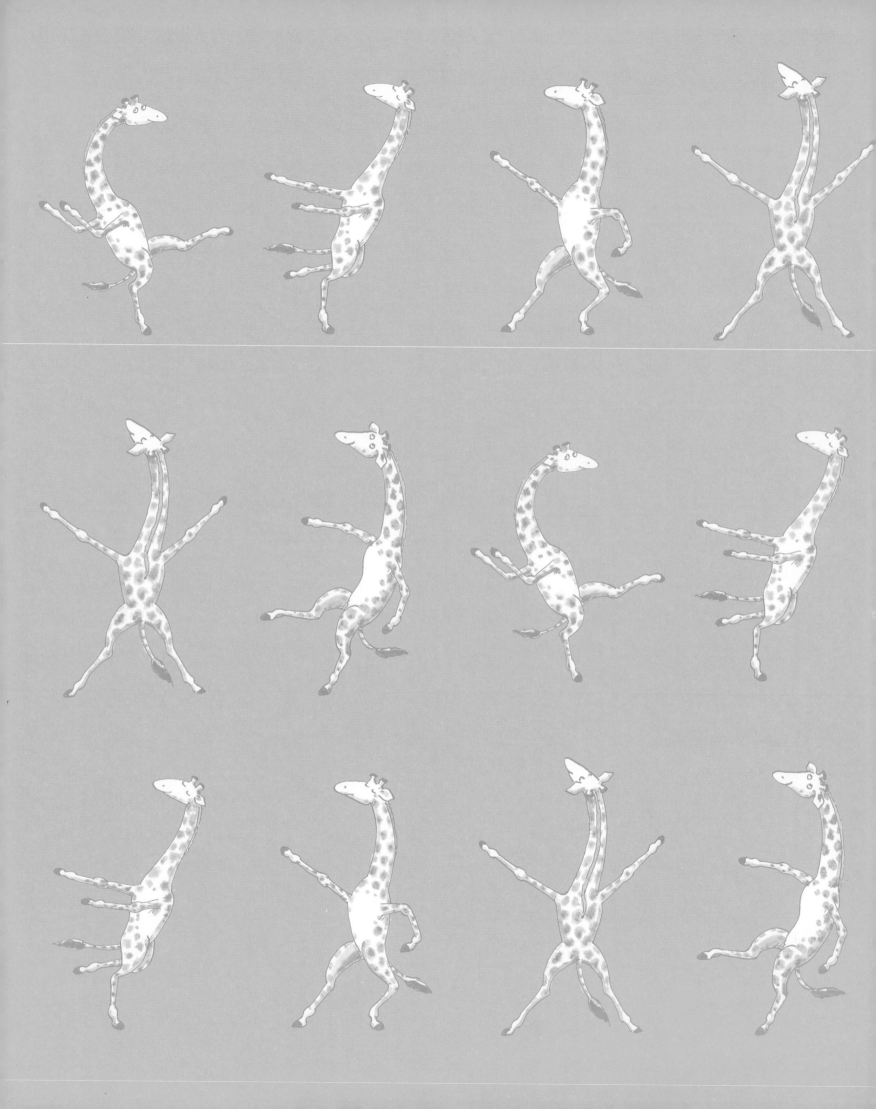